Persephone

and the
Pomegranate Seeds

First published in 2008 by
Franklin Watts
338 Euston Road
London
NW1 3BH

Franklin Watts Australia
Level 17/207 Kent Street
Sydney
NSW 2000

Text © Maggie Moore 2008
Illustration © Martin Impey 2008

A CIP catalogue record for this book is available
from the British Library.

ISBN 978 0 7496 7995 8 (hbk)
ISBN 978 0 7496 8003 9 (pbk)

Series Editor: Melanie Palmer
Series Advisor: Dr Barrie Wade
Series Designer: Peter Scoulding

Printed in China

Franklin Watts is a division of
Hachette Children's Books,
an Hachette Livre UK company
www.hachettelivre.co.uk

HOPSCOTCH MYTHS

Persephone
and the
Pomegranate Seeds

by Maggie Moore and Martin Impey

W
FRANKLIN WATTS
LONDON•SYDNEY

Demeter was the goddess of
everything that grew on Earth.

Her daughter, Persephone, was beautiful. All the gods admired her. She helped her mother to cover the Earth with plants and flowers.

7

One day, Persephone was out
picking flowers for her mother.

At the same time, the god Hades
went out for a ride in his chariot.

As soon as Hades saw Persephone, he fell in love. He grabbed her and sped back down to his kingdom in the underworld.

"Welcome to the underworld," said
Hades. "Now you must stay here
and be my queen."

Persephone stamped her foot.

"No, I won't," she yelled.

"My mother needs me on Earth."

The underworld was cold, dark and lonely. Persephone missed the warm, bright sun and her friends on Earth.

15

"I know you miss the Earth,"
said Hades. "If you eat some of
this fruit, you will feel better."

But Persephone refused.

She was too sad to eat.

Back on Earth, Demeter looked
everywhere for Persephone.

No one had seen her, not even the
shepherd. She was so sad that she
forgot to look after the plants and
they started to die.

Soon there were no flowers. There
was no fruit and no corn. The
people on Earth began to starve.

Zeus, king of the gods, saw that the
Earth was bare. He sent Hermes,
his messenger, to find Persephone.

In the underworld, Hades tried once more to make Persephone eat. He knew that if she did, she would have to stay with him forever.

"Please eat this pomegranate," he begged her. "If you do, you can see your mother again," he lied.

So Persephone ate just four
of the pomegranate seeds.
"At last!" cried Hades, dancing
with joy. "Now you must stay here!"

Just then Hermes arrived, but he
was too late. "Don't eat anything
else!" he cried. Then he rushed
back to tell Demeter.

Demeter was furious. "Nothing
will grow on Earth while
Persephone is in the underworld,"
she told Zeus, angrily.

So Zeus thought of a plan. He sent
Hermes to bring Persephone to him.

"As you have eaten four seeds,
you must stay in the underworld
for four months each year,"
Zeus told Persephone.

"But for the other months of the year, you can be with me on Earth," said her mother, Demeter.

So each year, when Persephone returns to the Earth, plants grow and corn ripens in the summer sun.

But when she goes down to the
underworld, plants freeze in winter's
cold. Nothing grows until her return
and the start of spring.

Hopscotch has been specially designed to fit the requirements of the Literacy Framework. It offers real books by top authors and illustrators for children developing their reading skills. There are 63 Hopscotch stories to choose from:

Marvin, the Blue Pig
ISBN 978 0 7496 4619 6

Plip and Plop
ISBN 978 0 7496 4620 2

The Queen's Dragon
ISBN 978 0 7496 4618 9

Flora McQuack
ISBN 978 0 7496 4621 9

Willie the Whale
ISBN 978 0 7496 4623 3

Naughty Nancy
ISBN 978 0 7496 4622 6

Run!
ISBN 978 0 7496 4705 6

The Playground Snake
ISBN 978 0 7496 4706 3

"Sausages!"
ISBN 978 0 7496 4707 0

Bear in Town
ISBN 978 0 7496 5875 5

Pippin's Big Jump
ISBN 978 0 7496 4710 0

Whose Birthday Is It?
ISBN 978 0 7496 4709 4

The Princess and the Frog
ISBN 978 0 7496 5129 9

Flynn Flies High
ISBN 978 0 7496 5130 5

Clever Cat
ISBN 978 0 7496 5131 2

Moo!
ISBN 978 0 7496 5332 3

Izzie's Idea
ISBN 978 0 7496 5334 7

Roly-poly Rice Ball
ISBN 978 0 7496 5333 0

I Can't Stand It!
ISBN 978 0 7496 5765 9

Cockerel's Big Egg
ISBN 978 0 7496 5767 3

How to Teach a Dragon Manners
ISBN 978 0 7496 5873 1

The Truth about those Billy Goats
ISBN 978 0 7496 5766 6

Marlowe's Mum and the Tree House
ISBN 978 0 7496 5874 8

The Truth about Hansel and Gretel
ISBN 978 0 7496 4708 7

The Best Den Everr
ISBN 978 0 7496 5876 2

ADVENTURES

Aladdin and the Lamp
ISBN 978 0 7496 6692 7

Blackbeard the Pirate
ISBN 978 0 7496 6690 3

George and the Dragon
ISBN 978 0 7496 6691 0

Jack the Giant-Killer
ISBN 978 0 7496 6693 4

TALES OF KING ARTHUR

1. The Sword in the Stone
ISBN 978 0 7496 6694 1

2. Arthur the King
ISBN 978 0 7496 6695 8

3. The Round Table
ISBN 978 0 7496 6697 2

4. Sir Lancelot and the Ice Castle
ISBN 978 0 7496 6698 9

TALES OF ROBIN HOOD

Robin and the Knight
ISBN 978 0 7496 6699 6

Robin and the Monk
ISBN 978 0 7496 6700 9

Robin and the Silver Arrow
ISBN 978 0 7496 6703 0

Robin and the Friar
ISBN 978 0 7496 6702 3

FAIRY TALES

The Emperor's New Clothes
ISBN 978 0 7496 7421 2

Cinderella
ISBN 978 0 7496 7417 5

Snow White
ISBN 978 0 7496 7418 2

Jack and the Beanstalk
ISBN 978 0 7496 7422 9

The Three Billy Goats Gruff
ISBN 978 0 7496 7420 5

The Pied Piper of Hamelin
ISBN 978 0 7496 7419 9

Goldilocks and the Three Bears
ISBN 978 0 7496 7903 3

Hansel and Gretel
ISBN 978 0 7496 7904 0

The Three Little Pigs
ISBN 978 0 7496 7905 7

Rapunzel
ISBN 978 0 7496 7906 4

Little Red Riding Hood
ISBN 978 0 7496 7907 1

Rumpelstiltskin
ISBN 978 0 7496 7908 8

HISTORIES

Toby and the Great Fire of London
ISBN 978 0 7496 7410 6

Pocahontas the Peacemaker
ISBN 978 0 7496 7411 3

Grandma's Seaside Bloomers
ISBN 978 0 7496 7412 0

Hoorah for Mary Seacole
ISBN 978 0 7496 7413 7

Remember the 5th of November
ISBN 978 0 7496 7414 4

Tutankhamun and the Golden Chariot
ISBN 978 0 7496 7415 1

MYTHS

Icarus, the Boy Who Flew
ISBN 978 0 7496 7992 7 *
ISBN 978 0 7496 8000 8

Perseus and the Snake Monster
ISBN 978 0 7496 7993 4 *
ISBN 978 0 7496 8001 5

Odysseus and the Wooden Horse
ISBN 978 0 7496 7994 1 *
ISBN 978 0 7496 8002 2

Persephone and the Pomegranate Seeds
ISBN 978 0 7496 7995 8 *
ISBN 978 0 7496 8003 9

Romulus and Remus
ISBN 978 0 7496 7996 5 *
ISBN 978 0 7496 8004 6

Thor's Hammer
ISBN 978 0 7496 7997 2*
ISBN 978 0 7496 8005 3

No Dinner for Anansi
ISBN 978 0 7496 7998 9 *
ISBN 978 0 7496 8006 0

Gelert the Brave
ISBN 978 0 7496 7999 6*
ISBN 978 0 7496 8007 7

* hardback